adapted by Jodie Shepherd
based on the teleplay written by Janice Burgess
illustrated by The Artifact Group

Ready-to-Read

SIMON SPOTLIGHT/NICKELODEON
New York   London   Toronto   Sydney

Based on the TV series *Nick Jr. The Backyardigans*™ as seen on Nick Jr.®

SIMON SPOTLIGHT
An imprint of Simon & Schuster Children's Publishing Division
1230 Avenue of the Americas, New York, New York 10020
© 2009 Viacom International Inc. All rights reserved.
NICK JR., *Nick Jr. The Backyardigans*, and all related titles, logos, and characters are trademarks
of Viacom International Inc. NELVANA™ Nelvana Limited. CORUS™ Corus Entertainment Inc.
SIMON SPOTLIGHT, READY-TO-READ, and colophon
are registered trademarks of Simon & Schuster, Inc.
Manufactured in the United States of America
First Edition
2 4 6 8 10 9 7 5 3 1
Library of Congress Cataloging-in-Publication Data
Shepherd, Jodie.
Robot rampage! / adapted by Jodie Shepherd ; illustrated by The Artifact Group. — 1st ed.
p. cm.
"Nickelodeon The Backyardigans."
ISBN 978-1-4169-9013-0
I. Artifact Group. II. Backyardigans (Television program) III. Title.
PZ7.S54373Ro 2009
[E]—dc22
2009008521

"How are you doing,
ROBOT

Roscoe?" asks Repairman  .
AUSTIN

"All systems A-OK,"

 Roscoe replies.
ROBOT

Repairman 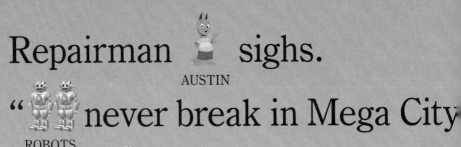 sighs.

AUSTIN

" never break in Mega City

ROBOTS

Every is always A-OK."

ROBOT

"And if  never ever break,"
ROBOTS

says Repairman ,
AUSTIN

"there is no work for me."

The  rings. It is .

PHONE   UNIQUA

"My  is broken," cries .

ROBOT   UNIQUA

"Please hurry!"

"Hooray!" says 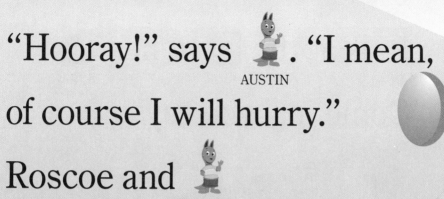 AUSTIN. "I mean, of course I will hurry."

Roscoe and AUSTIN

take off in their flying TRUCK.

is at the to her .

UNIQUA   DOOR   HOUSE

"Come in," she says.

" 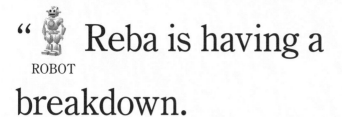 Reba is having a

breakdown.

I think she has a loose .

SCREW

Can you fix her?"

"I told her to make ," COOKIES

says . UNIQUA

"Now she will not stop.

She will not share, either.

My is on a rampage!" ROBOT

AUSTIN finally fixes the ROBOT.

No one sees the evil  PROFESSOR BUG.

No one notices that

the loose SCREW is alive!

"Help!" cries  from outside.
TYRONE

"I told my 🤖 to get the ✉,"
ROBOT **MAIL**

says 🫎.
TYRONE

"Now look at these 📮📮!"
MAILBOXES

Oh, no! Another  breakdown!

 chases the  and fixes it.

ROBOT
AUSTIN
ROBOT

The loose  flies into

SCREW

the hands of the evil  .

PROFESSOR BUG

Oh, no! Another 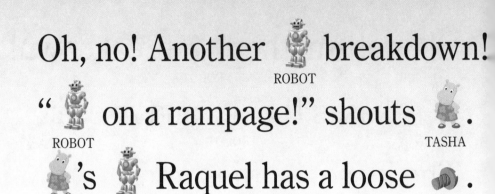 breakdown!
ROBOT

" on a rampage!" shouts .
ROBOT   TASHA

's Raquel has a loose .
TASHA   ROBOT   SCREW

She is on a rampage!

climbs into his .

AUSTIN   TRUCK

"Step on it, Roscoe!"

ROBOT

 fixes Raquel, too.

AUSTIN   ROBOT

But  **ROBOTS** are on a rampage all over town.

What is going on?

"People of Mega City," yells 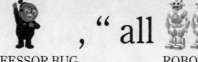 PROFESSOR BUG , " all ROBOTS are now in my control.

Ha, ha! No one can stop me!"

Whoa!

The loose from 🤖 Raquel

SCREW   ROBOT

is running away!

It is a 🔩 bug.

SCREW

🦘 grabs it.

AUSTIN

"That is how 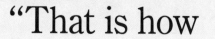 controls the !

He bugs them!"

 knows how to stop !

and his friends
AUSTIN

board the flying .
TRUCK

They go to the lab of .
PROFESSOR BUG

There are many guards.
ROBOT

How will they sneak into
the lab?

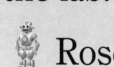 Roscoe knows! They will

act like !

ROBOT

ROBOTS

"Make way for !" says .

ICE CREAM AUSTIN

 loves .

PROFESSOR BUG ICE CREAM

 drops the   .

PROFESSOR BUG ROBOT REMOTE CONTROL

 grabs the .

PROFESSOR BUG ICE CREAM

grabs the .

AUSTIN ROBOT REMOTE CONTROL

"Three cheers for Repairman !" shout , , and .

AUSTIN UNIQUA TASHA TYRONE

"Your evil days are over, . Now help us fix all of

PROFESSOR BUG

the !"

ROBOTS

Rumble, rumble, rumble!

Are there more on

ROBOTS

a rampage?

"It is my stomach," says .

AUSTIN

"Time for some ICE CREAM !"